Badger Boy

Anthony Masters

Illustrated by **Joan-Marie Abley**

mammoth

*To the memory of Dr Ernest Neal, my companion
in badger watching. He was the world's most
distinguished badger expert and gave his knowledge
generously and with inspiration.*
A.M.

*With much love to my dad,
for having faith in my ability*
J-M.A.

The author would like to thank Michael Clark for his
expert advice

First published in Great Britain in 1999
by Mammoth, an imprint of Egmont Children's Books Limited
239 Kensington High Street, London, W8 6SA

Text copyright © 1999 Anthony Masters
Illustrations copyright © 1999 Joan-Marie Abley

The moral rights of the author and illustrator have been asserted

The rights of Anthony Masters and Joan-Marie Abley to be
identified as the author and illustrator of this work have
been asserted by them in accordance with the
Copyright, Designs and Patents Act 1988

ISBN 0 7497 3805 7

10 9 8 7 6 5 4 3 2

A CIP catalogue record for this book is
available from the British Library

Printed in Great Britain by Cox & Wyman Ltd,
Reading, Berkshire

Contents

CHAPTER ONE

The wood was gloomy and sinister at twilight, unnaturally silent as Kerry slowly approached.

She had only been in the countryside for twenty-four hours but she had already had more than enough of the dirty, scratchy, smelly place.

Red in tooth and claw. That's what Mum had told her when they had discovered the savaged corpse of a kitten at the back of the barn.

'A fox?' Kerry had whispered, but her

mother had only shrugged.

'And you thought it was rabbits with white mittens and sheepdogs with ribbons,' Mum had said.

'You've got the words muddled up,' Kerry had grumbled.

South Wimbledon might not have many trees, and the grass on the football field might always be dusty and dog stained, but at least you knew what to expect. In the country, life was less certain.

As Kerry pushed her way into the wood through tangled undergrowth and tightly packed trees covered in ivy, she felt her face catch in a large spider's web which stretched between two bushes across her path. She shuddered.

Kerry had been horrified when Mum had

told her that her aunt had been run over by a truck in front of her husband Paul and son Barry. She had never been to the West Country and could barely remember her relations there. Now she couldn't stop thinking of her cousin Barry without his mother. When Mum had suggested going down to stay with Paul and Barry, to help them through the tragedy, Kerry had been pleased.

'They don't have any other relations,' Mum had told her. 'We've got to support them at a time like this. It's bad enough for me. I hadn't seen Liz for years. But to lose his mother at his age – just like that. It doesn't bear thinking about.'

Kerry wanted to help Barry and hoped that, even at this terrible time, they would become friends. At twelve, Kerry was tall and good looking, but she'd suddenly lost her confidence. She'd just started a new school and was finding it difficult to make friends. Kerry had never had that problem before. What was the matter with her? Did her breath smell? Did she spit when she spoke? A few days away were more than welcome –

especially if she could help Barry too. But now the rescue mission to Somerset looked like being a failure. Uncle Paul had seemed pleased on the phone when Mum suggested coming down, but he had been quite surly when they arrived, as if he regretted the decision and hadn't been able to think of a way of putting them off.

A branch snapped back in her face and Kerry shuddered again as she gazed up at

the fungi clinging to the trunk of the tree. A breeze rustled the ivy and her thoughts uneasily returned to a story she had read about an enchanted wood where all the trees had once been human beings.

As Kerry pushed on, stumbling into a patch of nettles which stung her hand, she wondered whether her cousin and his father actually needed help. Barry had been out when she woke this morning, and he had ignored her at lunch. Kerry had tried not to stare, but even at a glance she could see his slate-grey eyes seemed mocking and hostile. He looked stubborn and distant and rather threatening.

As she stumbled on through the undergrowth, she noticed a pungent smell. It was wild garlic. Something soft and fluttery brushed her hair and Kerry bit back a scream. 'I hate this horrible wood,' she said.

Then Kerry saw him. Barry was leaning against a tree, completely still.

CHAPTER TWO

As Kerry gazed ahead the smell of raw earth blotted out the garlic. Earth. The word beat in her head. She had had a horror of that smell ever since a boy at playschool had rubbed her nose in the stuff when they had been on an outing to a local park. But her curiosity pushed the suffocating memory aside.

Barry was sitting so still that for a wild moment Kerry wondered if he was dead.

She was terrified, unable to move, frozen into the soil, the smell of earth overpowering.

Then she began to stumble towards him, cracking twigs.

There was another pungent, musky smell Kerry couldn't identify. Suddenly she could see a large clumsy-looking shape in the gathering darkness. Startled, she stepped back and tripped over a root, sprawling on the ground. As Kerry struggled to her feet, she was blinded by a flashlight.

'Idiot!'

'Turn that off,' wailed Kerry.

'You've ruined everything.' Barry swung the flashlight away.

There was a grunt and a scuffling sound. Straining her eyes, Kerry could just pick out stripes and then more creatures seemed to disappear into the earth.

'You idiot!' Barry muttered again, leaning

stiffly against the tree, staring at her furiously.

'I couldn't see anything. I could have broken my ankle.'

'Why did you follow me?'

'I didn't! I was looking for you.' Kerry was on the verge of tears. What *was* it about her? Why didn't people like her nowadays? 'What were those things?' she asked, trying to appease him. 'Foxes?'

'Of course they weren't. I've got to get back.' Barry pushed past her and was swallowed up in the darkness.

There was no path and Kerry looked round desperately. 'You can't leave me here,' she yelled.

'Why not?' But at least he was waiting and Kerry ran to catch up with him, almost falling over again. She felt a complete fool.

'What were you doing?'

'Watching badgers.' He paused. 'It was private.' There was a long silence. Then Barry said grudgingly, 'Come on.'

'Where?'

'Home, of course. You as thick as you look?'

Directly they reached the welcome warmth and light of the cottage, Barry went straight through the kitchen and upstairs to bed without speaking to anyone.

'Cocoa?' Mum asked in the bright voice she always used when she was under stress.

'Thanks.'

'Biscuit?' Despite the fact that he had run to fat, Paul still looked like his son and his slate-grey eyes seemed just as mocking. 'They're home-made.'

Kerry paused fractionally, wondering if she was eating a dead woman's biscuit.

'I baked them.' It was as if Paul had read her thoughts. 'Just a little hobby.'

'Barry's got one too – watching badgers,' Kerry blurted out.

'Did you see them?' asked Mum.

'Not really.' She ate another biscuit and choked slightly. 'I made a noise. They ran away.'

'He used to watch the badgers with his

mother,' said her uncle.

'Did he?' Kerry couldn't think of anything else to say.

'Do you watch them, Paul?' asked Mum, even more brightly.

'I haven't got the time.'

'I'm surprised Barry can bear to go in that wood on his own.'

Now her mother was being stupid. Kerry knew it was only because she was so nervous.

'Perhaps he thinks he's –' Kerry began and then stopped.

'Go on.' Paul sounded threatening.

'With her.' She stumbled to a halt.

'That's a good thing to say.' Her uncle's voice was suddenly warmer.

'Barry's got a lot of grieving to do,' said Mum in a hushed, reverent tone.

'Can I have another biscuit?' Kerry asked.

'Take as many as you like.' Her uncle pushed the tin across the table. His face suddenly crumpled.

Kerry lay in bed wondering what it would be like if her own mother or father died. She closed her eyes against the appalling idea and then opened them again. Paul and Barry had to live with that terrible grief every day of their lives. How *could* they cope with it? She wouldn't even know how to begin.

Then she heard sobbing.

Barry's bedroom was next to hers and Kerry opened her door a fraction to listen carefully. The sobbing seemed slightly more muffled now, as if he had turned over and buried his face in the pillow.

Downstairs she could hear the buzz of the television set and her uncle's voice.

Kerry didn't know what to do. She had already broken into Barry's privacy once and wrecked his badger watch. For a moment she hesitated. Then Kerry opened his bedroom door and went inside.

CHAPTER THREE

Kerry sensed a raw earthy smell and the room seemed deadly cold.

The sobbing was still muffled and she could see the dim shape of Barry's face pressed deep into the pillow.

She stood there uneasily.

'Barry?'

There was no reply.

She spoke louder. 'Barry?'

He stopped sobbing and lay still, as if he were a cornered animal wanting to hide but knowing there was nowhere to go. Then he rolled over on his back. 'Get out!'

She almost went, but instead remained standing by his bedside.

'Why don't you leave me alone?'

'I heard you – crying.'

'I wasn't crying.'

'Sobbing, then.'

He didn't reply.

'We're cousins,' she said desperately.

'What difference does that make? I'd never even met you before – ' He didn't finish the sentence.

Now that her eyes were getting used to the dark, Kerry spotted a letter flattened out on the duvet. 'What's that?' It was typed and official looking.

'You're nosy, aren't you?' He snatched up the letter and flung it at her. Then, unexpectedly, he picked up the flashlight so that she could see to read. Kerry was so surprised that she almost didn't react. Barry was going to share something with her. Something big. She *had* to be up to it.

```
Dear Mr Cole,

This is to inform you that Dakers
Wood is now closed to the public
as I will shortly be cutting and
selling the timber.

Yours sincerely,
Andrew Mason.
```

'Is that where the badgers live?'

Barry nodded. 'Mason owns the wood.' His voice was low, on one note.

'Who is he?'

'A stranger. Only moved in a few months ago. We haven't seen anything of him – and we don't want to.'

'Has your father read this letter?'

'Not yet.'

'It's addressed to him.'

'So what?' Barry gave her the envelope which was marked 'Urgent'. 'I didn't want Dad to see anything upsetting. Anything marked urgent seems upsetting to me.'

'You could have talked it over.' Kerry knew she was pushing Barry away again. 'What about the other farmer? The one before Mason?'

'Jack Soames retired. He didn't mind us watching the badgers.'

'Who's us?'

'Me and Mum.'

He looked away and Kerry knew there were tears in his eyes. She felt useless. She didn't know how to reach him. But if only she could . . .

'Why don't you fight?' she eventually blurted out.

'Who?' For the first time he looked marginally interested in what Kerry had to say. She seized on it.

'When the council tried to close the adventure playground in the park at home, we fought and won.'

'How?'

'Petitions. Demonstrations –'

'Mason can do what he likes with his own wood.' Barry's eyes were fixed on Kerry's, challenging her to find a solution.

'We could try to make a protest,' she suggested, not wanting to let this breakthrough slip away, but he seemed to have lost interest in what she was saying. He was staring at the wall.

Then he said, 'There's this boy at school.'

'What about him?'

'His dad runs ARC.'

'What's that?' Kerry's voice was dull. She felt she was being pushed away again, that Barry was about to turn to someone else.

'Animal Rights in the Countryside.'

'So?'

'Badgers have rights, don't they? Maybe ARC would make a protest.'

'They might,' said Kerry cautiously, trying to respond. Was there a place for her in all this? Then she felt ashamed. Why was she being so selfish? 'Don't you think you should show that letter to your dad?' Kerry knew she sounded patronising, but she had always had her own sense of 'rightness', and she couldn't go against that even for the sake of pleasing Barry.

'I'll show him tomorrow.' He looked more relaxed, more purposeful, as if he could stop thinking and start doing.

But Kerry still felt excluded.

'Will you tell your father about ARC?'

'Sure.' He sounded quite reasonable now. Then came the big surprise. 'Why don't you come and watch the badgers tomorrow night?'

'The wood's closed.'

'Not to me.'

'But the letter said – I mean – won't we get into trouble?'

Barry looked at her contemptuously. 'If you're scared, don't bother.'

'I'll come,' said Kerry, too abruptly, too eagerly.

He drew the duvet up to his neck and turned on his side.

Kerry was so tired that when she got back to her own bed she instantly plunged into deep and dreamless sleep, and woke late. Hurrying downstairs she found only her mother at the breakfast table. There was no sign of Paul or Barry.

'They've gone to Linton market.' Mum

seemed depressed.

'And deliberately left us behind.'

'I thought it would be better if they spent some time alone.'

Kerry could see that her mother was also hurt about them going off together. She knew she was thinking that they'd dropped everything to come all this way to look after

Paul and Barry, who now didn't want – or need – to be looked after.

A sense of injustice swept over Kerry, followed by a wave of homesickness. She thought about Dad fending for himself all on his own, and her mother feeling guilty about not having seen her sister for so long. If only Paul had stopped them coming.

'Did Barry tell his father about the letter?'

'What letter?'

Kerry explained what had happened during the night. When she had finished there was a long silence.

'You're a good girl, Kerry.'

'Am I?'

'At least you've got through to Barry, which is more than I have. But this ARC business worries me.'

'How soon are we going home?'

'Sunday. Barry's going back to school on Monday.'

'He's asked me to go badger watching tonight.'

'You said the wood's closed.' Mum sounded anxious.

'Barry won't worry about that.'

'Suppose the farmer turns up?'

'We'll apologise.'

'He might call the police.'

Kerry shrugged. 'This is important, Mum.'

'That boy's been running wild down here for years. I hope he's not going to get you into trouble.'

'I want to be friends with him. That's what I was meant to do, wasn't it? That's why you wanted me to come down here in the first place.'

'I thought you might help him,' said her mother. 'And it might do you some good, too.'

'How's that?' asked Kerry defensively, guessing what she meant but ashamed that she knew.

'I know you're not happy at school. Maybe Dad and I shouldn't have pushed St Luke's so hard. You could have gone to Beldan High where all your friends went. It's just that we thought St Luke's was a better school and you'd soon settle down, and –'

'Mum,' Kerry interrupted, not wanting her to go on any longer. 'Why *haven't* you brought me here before?'

Her mother looked away. 'Liz and I quarrelled about your gran going into a home. Liz wanted Gran to stay with her in the country for six months and with us for the rest of the year. But we've got such a small house and Gran was ill . . .'

'Isn't she happy at The Beeches?'

'I think she is.' Her mother deliberately changed the subject. 'Anyway, I don't want you trespassing in that wood.'

'If I don't go, he'll never speak to me again.'

Her mother sighed and then gave in. 'Just this once, mind.'

CHAPTER FOUR

Kerry spent the rest of the day lying in the long grass of the overgrown back garden, reading, getting too hot in the sun, willing Barry to come home. But the hours dragged by and she became increasingly drowsy and irritable.

Mum was busy cleaning the house, and Kerry felt guilty when she finally emerged with a dishcloth in her hand.

'You'll be careful, won't you?'

'Of course,' Kerry snapped.

'And I don't mean with the farmer.'

'What *do* you mean, then?'

'Barry.'

'I don't understand.'

Her mother was gazing down at her. 'That boy's in a very bad emotional state,' she said. 'And so is his dad. I'm worried you'll get hurt.'

Barry and Paul arrived back in the pick-up looking strained. Barry ran up to his room without speaking and Kerry returned miserably to the garden. She listened to Paul's and Mum's voices through the open kitchen window.

'How did it go?' her mother asked him.

'OK.' Her uncle sounded exhausted.

'How was Barry?'

'OK.'

'Did you have a row?'

'No.'

'I just wondered –'

Kerry closed her eyes, knowing her mother was pushing her luck. She never went slowly enough . . .

'Don't bother.'

'Sorry?'

'What happened between me and Barry is –'

'Private.' She was quick to make amends. 'I didn't mean to pry.'

'I'm going to do some work in the shed.'

'What time do you want supper?'

'Any time.'

Kerry felt indignant on her mother's behalf. 'Why are you being so rude?' she wanted to shout. 'We're only trying to help.'

But Kerry kept these thoughts to herself. She knew the Coles didn't want their help.

'Coming?'

She hadn't noticed Barry standing beside her and Kerry got to her feet feeling flustered.

'You do realise you have to keep quiet,' he said sternly.

'Of course.'

'And still.'

'Yes –'

'And do exactly what I say.'

'OK.' Kerry resented the instructions. She made

up her mind not to let Barry get away with bossing her round again.

Kerry didn't find the wood so frightening this time. She was enjoying being with Barry and he obviously felt quite at home there. The garlic smell was less strong and she noticed wild flowers that seemed comforting and almost inviting.

'Don't step on any twigs,' hissed Barry.

'I'm not that stupid.'

'You were last night.'

'I was scared and I was alone. I bet there'd be things in a town you'd be –'

'Shut up.'

'Don't you dare speak to me like that!'

'If you don't shut up, I'll call off the watch.'

'Who do you think you are?'

Barry ignored her and Kerry kept morosely quiet as they continued to pick their way through the tangled undergrowth, eventually arriving in a clearing.

'Get in front of one of those oaks.'

'Don't you mean behind?'

'I mean what I say,' snapped Barry.

Kerry grudgingly did as she was told while he leant against the tree beside her.

'You've got to swallow yourself.'

'*What*?'

'It's a kind of trick that keeps you still.'

'I don't understand.'

'Take a deep breath – and swallow until you feel you've disappeared. Then lean against the tree and don't move at all. We could be in for a long wait.'

Kerry took a deep breath and in her mind's

eye saw her mouth growing enormous, a huge hole through which her body might travel with ease.

It was the most extraordinary feeling – as if she had disappeared completely and was just a sliver of evening mist settled against the soft and yielding bark. She hadn't the slightest desire to scratch, cough or clear her throat.

Barry had worked some kind of miracle.

CHAPTER FIVE

Kerry felt part of the night itself and was amazed by the acuteness of her hearing, each sound crystal clear. A bird sang, a small animal scurried across the glade, a rabbit appeared sniffing the wind, an owl hooted and there was a series of short, sharp barks from some way away.

Soon a full moon
rode the night sky
and Kerry could
smell the musky
scent again, but it was
no longer threatening. A snuffling
sound came from some large holes in the
opposite bank. She watched intently,
unconscious of the passing of time until a
snout appeared, sniffing the air as the badger
came out, cautiously looking round.

Satisfied that all was safe, the creature
began to tread slowly across the glade. Then
another snout emerged, and a smaller,
sleeker badger appeared. They began to
scratch and nibble at their fur and then to
groom each other with small, delighted
whickering sounds.

Suddenly there was a scrabbling rush and three cubs burst out of the hole, much smaller than their parents, with soft, fluffy fur, running about in the long grass, leap-frogging each other, closely watched by the sow while the boar ambled out of sight.

The cubs began to roll about on the ground, snarling, whickering, yelping and grunting as they chewed at each other's ears and necks. Then one of them jumped up on a fallen tree trunk and played King of the Castle as the others tried to push it off. When

one cub fell, another took its place and the game started all over again, only to end abruptly when the sow began to move away. For a moment her cubs stood uneasily still and then hurriedly began to follow.

After a while, Barry moved and Kerry was suddenly aware of being stiff and cold. The magic had gone.

'We'd better get going,' he said.

'It was fantastic.' Her voice sounded wrong, ugly in the night air.

'There are more badgers in the sett – maybe another ten.'

'Where have this lot gone?' She didn't *want* to talk. Kerry wanted to swallow herself again, to return to the enchantment.

'To hunt for food. They'll be back by

dawn.' Barry switched the flashlight on. 'Hurry up – I've got to call Tim.' He sounded dismissive.

'Who's Tim?'

'The boy whose father runs the local branch of ARC.'

'Is he a good friend of yours?'

Barry only gave an irritating laugh, but as he did so, another flashlight could be seen, weaving through the undergrowth towards them.

Kerry had a surge of panic and felt Barry stiffen beside her.

'What do you think you're up to?' A man's dark shadow spread like a giant bat.

'Badger watching,' said Barry casually.

'The wood belongs to me now and it's closed. You're trespassing.'

'What's your name?' asked Barry aggressively, and Kerry noticed that he was standing with his fists clenched, shaking slightly.

'Andrew Mason.'

'Jack Soames would never have done this.'

'Wait a minute.' The farmer paused and then continued more hesitantly. 'Didn't I send your father a letter saying this wood is closed to the public?' His voice softened. 'And aren't you the boy who lost his mother?'

'It's none of your business.' Barry's voice broke and Kerry felt his pain, hard and cold.

There was a long silence. Then Mason said stiffly, 'The wood's closed. I'm chopping it down.'

'Why?' asked Kerry.

'Farming's going through a bad patch. You can't just rely on the milk cheque now. The only way to make a farm pay is to diversify, so I need to sell the timber. I'm not expecting you kids to understand my problems. Why should you? But there's plenty of other badger setts in the valley.'

'He used to watch in this wood. With his mother.' Kerry wanted to explain. But she was not given a chance.

'Don't patronise me!' Barry yelled at her as he ran off.

They watched him go, flashlight bobbing, unerringly finding his way through the undergrowth, like a Will o' the Wisp.

'He's had a terrible shock,' said Kerry miserably, knowing everything had slipped out of control.

CHAPTER SIX

'Someone needs to keep an eye on him,' said Andrew Mason uneasily. Then he added, 'I've got the timber people coming in a couple of days.'

'Where will the badgers go?' Kerry asked.

'I don't know,' he admitted. 'The trouble is they're territorial. They'll be attacked if they try to invade another sett so I guess they'll just have to fend for themselves and start digging.'

'On your land?'

Andrew Mason only shrugged. 'Do you

know your way back?'

'Of course.' She felt uncomfortable getting close to the enemy, however civilised he might be.

He looked at her. 'You'd better follow me.'

'I'm OK.'

'Don't be stupid.'

Kerry suddenly realised she was being just that. She would never have found her way back.

For a while they walked in silence, Mason leading the way with his flashlight.

'I'm sorry,' he said at last. 'I wish I could be more helpful.'

'I know you can't,' she replied flatly.

'He'll find another wood.'

'You're wrong,' she snapped, seeing the lights of the cottage and running past him.

'He'll never find a wood which means so much to him.'

Kerry went up to her room, tired and cold and wanting to be alone. Barry was waiting for her on the landing.

'I just spoke to Tim. ARC are going to occupy the wood tomorrow morning.' He was triumphant. 'That'll teach Mason a lesson.'

'Just like that?' Kerry was scoffing. She felt excluded.

'I spoke to Tim's father.'

'And has he spoken to yours?'

'Why do you always want everything fixed up by adults?'

'*Have* you told your father?' she demanded stubbornly, determined to be practical however much she really wanted to side with

Barry.

'As a matter of fact I have.'

'You really think they'll be able to stop Mason?'

'You bet they will.'

'And you're going to join the protest?'

'I'm going to earth,' Barry replied mysteriously.

'I'm all for this protest,' said her uncle as they drank coffee round the kitchen table. 'I don't see why Mason should get away with vandalism. No one should be allowed to chop down a whole wood. Personally I'm proud of Barry. At least he's got some get up and go.'

Kerry was surprised at his reaction. She had expected him to be more cautious. Then she felt scared. What had Barry meant when he said, 'I'm going to earth'?

'I don't like this Mason character at all,' Paul continued. 'Dear old Jack Soames was a real friend to us – and the badgers. Used to watch them himself.'

'Andrew Mason didn't seem too bad to me,' said Kerry.

'So you'll welcome the protestors?' Mum asked Paul.

'As long as they don't break the law.'

'They'll be trespassing on Mason's land.'

Suddenly Kerry loved her for being so outspoken. She wouldn't suck up to anyone either, however unpopular she got. They were similar in that way.

'Oh I don't regard trespassing as breaking the law,' her uncle snapped. 'We've all got our rights, including the badgers.'

Like father, like son, Kerry thought as she went up to bed. They had both developed a real knack for making her and Mum feel stupid.

CHAPTER SEVEN

Kerry couldn't get to sleep that night, tossing and turning and worrying about Barry. Eventually she drifted off, only to dream that she was back in the wood again, waiting for the badgers to appear, flattened downwind against the tree.

In the stillness she swallowed herself and became mist on the bark of the tree. Then she heard a grunt and a whickering sound, but she could see no sign of Barry in the clear, bright moonlight. Instead, a large badger was shuffling through last autumn's dead leaves, his rank smell overpowering.

Kerry woke sweating and glanced at her watch. Six o'clock. A steel-grey dawn was creeping across the sky and she knew she had to get up.

Her bedroom window overlooked the ragged grass that rippled down the valley to where the wood began, and as she pulled back her curtains she saw a shadow detach itself from the trees, short and stocky and unmistakably Barry. He had a large spade over his shoulder and was wearing an old, baggy boiler

suit. When he came nearer she could see that he was covered in mud.

Kerry got dressed and trod warily to the half-open kitchen door. Barry was standing drinking tea, now in jeans and a T-shirt.

'What do you want?' he asked.

'I couldn't sleep.'

'So you spied on me,' said Barry.

Kerry gazed at him blankly.

'I saw you at the window,' he persisted.

'I *wasn't* spying on you.'

'OK.' He seemed exhausted, not wanting to argue any longer.

'Where have you been?'

'I thought you weren't spying.' Barry paused ungraciously. 'I've been down in the woods.'

'Doing what?'

'Going to earth.' He chuckled, and for a terrible moment Kerry wondered if the shock of his mother's death followed by the threat to the badgers had unhinged him. 'I've got a plan,' he said.

'What is it?'

'You'll only spoil it.'

She was bitterly hurt. 'Of course I won't.' Tears were welling up in her eyes.

'Wait a minute. I didn't mean that.'

'You did.'

There was a rumbling sound and they both hurried to the kitchen window. A large truck and a beaten-up old bus were trundling along the track that ran down beside the house to the wood. Both vehicles were painted light green and had the words ANIMAL

RIGHTS IN THE COUNTRYSIDE – ARC crudely stencilled on their sides.

Barry grinned. 'I'm off then.' He was packing food into a rucksack, together with a couple of bottles of orange squash, Mars bars and a small photograph of his mother that he had taken from the sideboard.

Kerry was about to ask if his father knew what he was going to do and then stopped herself. Instead she said, 'So you're going to sleep rough?'

Barry picked up his rucksack and paused. 'Will you be coming?' he asked.

There was no way of telling whether he wanted her to come or not. Kerry decided to lighten up and make a joke.

'I'll visit for the day, remembering to bring some sensible Wellington boots and a warm coat.'

'Suit yourself.'

CHAPTER EIGHT

The rain started slowly and soon became torrential. Kerry went back to bed with a buzzing headache and a feeling of inadequacy. She should have insisted on going with Barry. She was a wimp. A wimpess.

Suddenly Kerry wanted to be with Barry watching badgers more than anything in the world. She kept remembering how she had swallowed herself, becoming mist on bark. Barry had taught her that. Barry was magic.

Later, sitting at the breakfast table with

Mum and Paul, she built herself up to ask the obvious question. 'Can I go down to the wood?'

'I don't see why not,' said her uncle.

'Well –' her mother began cautiously.

'We'll all go down.' Paul was brisk. 'I want ARC to know how much I appreciate their protest. I could put a stand-pipe down there if needs be. Carting water about could be a problem.'

'What about Barry?' asked her mother. 'Are you going to let him camp out in this weather?'

'I think it'll distract him. Particularly now.'

'What do you mean – now?'

'I had a call from the police yesterday. The *post mortem*'s been completed so we must organise the funeral.'

'Does Barry know?' Kerry asked softly.

'Yes.'

'How did he take it?'

'By concentrating on the protest,' Paul said dismissively.

Mum sighed.

Kerry walked down into the wood, flanked by her mother and uncle. She expected a group of hippies or New Age travellers but instead the members of ARC were middle-aged men and women wearing anoraks. She was disappointed.

In the clearing near the badger sett they had erected a couple of large army-tents and her disappointment increased when she saw there were no tree-houses or rope bridges. Barry was nowhere to be seen.

There must have been about forty people in all, including a few teenagers who were quietly putting up tame, crudely painted placards that read SAVE THE BADGER SETTS.

As they looked round, a nervous, clean-shaven man with a thin, indoor face approached them.

'Can I help? The name's Trevor Hadfield.'

He doesn't look as if he could say boo to a goose, thought Kerry impatiently. Is this going to be a protest or a damp squib? The rain had stopped and there was a misty greyness.

'Paul Cole – and this is my sister-in-law Jill, and her daughter Kerry. We live up at the smallholding – or at least my son and I do. Jill and Kerry are just visiting.'

'You'll be Barry's father – the boy who kick-started the protest.' Trevor Hadfield paused. 'I was very sorry to hear about your wife's death. You must be –'

'Barry's concerned about the badgers.' Paul cut across the embarrassing sympathy.

'But he's very sensible,' added her mother.

Kerry grinned inwardly. How furious Barry would have been if he had heard that description.

'Do you think you'll have any effect?' Mum continued, putting into words exactly what Kerry was thinking.

'We're just a holding action while we try and get a Tree Preservation Order slapped on the wood. And, of course, it's illegal to damage a badger sett,' said Trevor Hadfield cautiously.

'You mean there's hope?' asked Paul eagerly.

'We'll just have to wait and see.'

'Has Mason been down?'

'No. I don't think he's got wind of us yet.'

'Where's Barry?' asked Kerry impatiently.

'He's gone off with my son Tim. Not quite sure what they're up to.'

Gone to earth. The ominous phrase repeated itself in Kerry's mind and her anxiety resurfaced.

Barry arrived with Tim a few minutes later. The wood was muddy and they seemed muddier. Tim was at least a couple of years older than her and Barry and had an air of dominance that Kerry didn't like, but she could see why Barry had been drawn to Tim

and felt a twinge of jealousy. At least he was
closer to how she thought a protestor *should*
look, with dirty blond hair flopping round his
shoulders, his nose pierced with a stud. He
also had an arrogance about him that was a

big contrast to his placid, anoraked father.

'Look at those two,' said Trevor. 'Talk about mudlarks.'

Kerry winced. She noticed that Barry didn't look too happy either. Perhaps, like her, he was wondering just how seriously he could take Trevor Hadfield. Maybe what they *really* needed were the motorway protestors, with their New Age clothes and long hair, to pep things up a bit.

'Barry's got it all sewn up,' Tim was telling his father. 'You ought to see what he's been up to.'

'Up to?' asked Paul, for once suspicious himself.

'Nothing, Dad.' Barry glared at Tim like he usually glared at Kerry.

'We've dug this big hole for an outdoor

toilet,' said Tim hastily. 'Barry's been working at it for ages so we can get more protestors on the site.'

Tim's too glib, thought Kerry. He's covering up . . .

'Won't that be really messing up Mr Mason's land?' Mum was upset and Kerry realised that she had come to respect the countryside, to see it as a real place that needed protecting.

'We'll come and take a look later,' said Trevor hurriedly.

The adults began to move away, talking amongst themselves.

'Can I have a look at your lav?' asked Kerry, trying to be funny again and failing miserably.

'No way.' Tim was dismissive.

'Why not?' She turned to Barry.

'You're not to blab to anyone,' he said reluctantly.

'She'll tell your dad,' warned Tim.

'She knows better than that,' said Barry fiercely.

Kerry felt a warm glow of acceptance and then a rush of irritation. She had never felt such complicated emotions before. Nor such creeping anxiety. What had Barry been doing?

CHAPTER NINE

When they arrived in the next glade, all
Kerry's worst fears were realised.

'What is it?' she demanded.

'It's a sett.' Barry pointed at the deep hole
in the bank.

Tim looked admiring, and Kerry frowned,
feeling Tim to be a rival.

'Barry's certainly had a brilliant idea,' Tim
said.

'Did you help him dig?' snapped Kerry.

'He'd done most of it already.'

'I've got wooden props in there. Can't you

see?' Barry was his usual scornful self.

Kerry bent down and peered into the hole

which sloped downwards, just like a badger's

sett. Suddenly the whole idea of Barry 'going to earth' filled her with terror. She *had* to stop him.

'You can't go down there.'

'He knows what he's doing.' Tim was at his most patronising. 'So why don't you push off?'

Kerry knew she risked her fragile friendship with Barry, but what he was doing was dangerous and she'd never respect herself again if she didn't intervene. 'We've got to stop him.'

'Tim's right. Why *don't* you push off?' Barry's fists were clenched and his face was white with rage. For a moment she wondered if he was going to hit her.

'What's the point of it all?' she asked defensively.

'I'm going to earth until Mason backs off. He'll have to dig me out.' Barry paused, grinning at Tim, unclenching his fists and beginning to calm down.

Then he went back to the sett and began to wriggle down the hole, eventually disappearing from sight.

'Go on,' said Tim. 'Do what he says. Go back to the others. Go back to Mummy.'

'If the rain starts again, all that earth could collapse,' Kerry persisted.

'It's only a protest,' snarled Tim. 'Barry knows what he's doing. And if you grass him up, he'll never speak to you for the rest of your life.'

Kerry thought that Tim was probably right.

CHAPTER TEN

As she feared, the rain started lashing down again when Kerry rejoined the protestors, leaving Tim and Barry on their own. She had decided she would tell her mother about what Barry had done, whatever the consequences, but Andrew Mason had arrived and was having a furious row with Trevor Hadfield.

'You get off my land now,' Mason was yelling.

'I've told you before,' persisted Trevor. 'We're not leaving until that Preservation Order comes through. Until we get that –'

Kerry noticed her mother and uncle were talking with the other demonstrators just outside one of the tents. She suddenly felt a rush of pride for Mum who was looking extremely determined. Kerry was sure that she wanted to campaign not just for Paul and Barry but also because of her sister and the quarrel they never made up.

'It's not fair,' Kerry heard her mother saying to Paul. 'The countryside belongs to everyone.'

Kerry noticed her uncle glance at Mum with a new respect.

Kerry saw Andrew Mason striding away and suddenly felt sorry for him. He seemed vulnerable with so many people against him, and she remembered how he had led her safely out of the wood the other evening.

Spontaneously, she ran after him and grabbed his arm. 'Couldn't you cut *half* the wood down and leave the sett?' she pleaded.

Mason was impatient. 'I need the timber. All of it. Every bit of my land has to earn money. I don't have a choice. I've got a family to look after.' He had stopped and they were both gazing back at the sett.

The rain was still teeming down and Kerry could smell wet, pungent earth. Then she heard shouting and the raw fear welled up inside her.

Tim was running towards them down the path. 'The sett's collapsed,' he yelled. 'You've got to come. He's gone and buried himself.'

Kerry felt a freezing cold sensation inside.

'Pull yourself together, Tim,' said his father slowly and patiently. 'What's happened?'

'It's collapsed.'

'What has?'

'The sett. Barry's sett.'

Paul Cole was staring at Tim in bewilderment. Mum gazed at Kerry, horrified.

'I was told he'd built a lavatory.' Paul sounded so indignant that Kerry felt hysterical laughter building up inside her.

Then the fear returned, cold and clutching. Barry was under the earth and she hadn't warned anyone.

In her mind's eye, Kerry saw him slipping the photograph of his mother into his bag.

They were both dead now.

CHAPTER ELEVEN

Kerry was in the lead as they all stumbled down the muddy path, slipping and sliding.

When she glanced back there were people everywhere, the mud tugging at their feet as if the earth itself was trying to slow them up.

Kerry's heart was thumping so painfully that she could barely breathe. Tim was weak, just a flashy show-off. It was she who was to blame.

'It must have collapsed on top of him,' gasped Tim.

All the time she was running, all the time

the mud seemed to be slowing her down, one single thought pounded in Kerry's head: *He's dead, like his mother. Dead like his mother. Dead like —*

When they got to the glade she could see that the bank Barry had spent so long digging into had collapsed on itself and there was no sign of any hole. It was as if a tomb had been sealed.

Some protestors had brought spades and they began to dig furiously.

Kerry glanced back to see that her mother had her arms round her uncle. 'Is there a chance?' she asked, not addressing anyone in particular.

'If we can get to him fast enough,' said Andrew Mason, sounding for once oddly ineffective. 'We'd better call an ambulance. But they'll take some time getting down here.'

Trevor dragged a mobile phone out of his pocket.

Barry was amazed he could still breathe. He was face-down, with a huge weight crushing his back.

Despite the pain, he had managed to grab the photograph of his mother which had been lying beside him. In the darkness he could feel that the glass was cracked, but that didn't matter. She was still with him.

So far he had felt too numb to panic, but he knew he daren't move in case he brought more earth down, and he gradually acknowledged the total stupidity of what he had done.

Suddenly Barry realised that he was breathing in a scent that he recognised but couldn't place. The smell was musky. The smell was badger, but with it came a stream of glorious fresh air.

* ★ ★ ★

Someone had brought more spades and Trevor, Paul, Mason, Mum and Tim had joined in the digging, panting, gasping, not pausing for a second. Kerry had tried to grab one but had been pushed away.

Feeling rejected and utterly useless, she stood hopelessly watching.

'I'm praying,' gasped Mum, tearing at the ground with her shovel. 'You pray too.'

Suddenly the earth Barry was lying on began to move and he hugged his mother's photograph to him as he began to drop, coming to rest a few metres below.

At first he thought the mud above him would fall in too and he'd be buried again, but nothing happened. The musky smell was much stronger now.

Stretching out, sore and aching, Barry began to feel more hopeful. He could see nothing in the pitch darkness but at least the pressure was off his back and he could move.

Then he froze as he touched something stiff and cold.

'Barry!' shouted Paul as he leant over the hole they had dug in the mound. 'Can you hear me?'

Everyone listened intently, but there was no reply.

'I'll have to get a digger,' muttered Andrew Mason.

'Do you think we've lost him?' Paul's voice shook.

'No,' said Trevor calmly. 'There could easily

be an air pocket.'

'That's right.' Kerry was determined to be hopeful. 'There *could* be an air pocket.' Her voice seemed to ring harshly, like an over-enthusiastic child.

Paul glanced across at Kerry. 'Want to have a go?'

She hurried across, grabbed the spade and began to work as hard and as fast as she could, but she made little impression. As she struggled, Kerry wondered if she had only been given the job because her uncle had finally accepted that Barry was dead. It was her fault. She had been too slow.

The corpse was cold but Barry didn't think the badger had been dead for long. He knew they usually walled up their dead in underground burial chambers, so was he in one of those chambers now? Then Barry breathed fresh air again – a definite current this time – and began to move slowly and painfully towards its source.

Suddenly he heard a muffled sound from above, but when he tried to squeeze his way up the tunnel he found the passage too narrow. Panic swept him as he clutched at his mother's photograph. Suppose the fresh air ran out? He would suffocate and that would be an awful way of dying – maybe even worse than Mum's.

Was there any point in calling for help? Barry didn't think so. But maybe he should try.

'Barry? Can you hear me?' yelled Tim. 'Barry?'

There was a long silence. Then Kerry heard something thin and distant yet familiar and she threw herself down, flattening her ear to the cold earth.

She began to tear at the ground with her bare hands and Trevor and Paul and Mum and Tim all began to dig again, this time with an even greater fury.

'He's got to be OK,' gasped Tim. 'He's got to be.'

The rain poured down and the pit they had dug filled with water.

'We've got to work harder than this.' Kerry was crouched down, still scraping at the earth, not noticing she was breaking her nails. Tim was doing the same.

Suddenly she found the mud was falling through a thin shaft and alternating waves of hope and despair swept through her.

As she grasped something muddy and sharp, she cut her hand, seeing the bright red blood seep down the jagged glass of the battered, mud-streaked frame that Barry was still holding.

'She's got him!' yelled Tim.

Paul fell to his knees in the puddle of mud and with Andrew Mason's help began to gently scoop at the soil until Barry's head and shoulders were freed.

Kerry kept talking softly to him. 'You're going to be all right now. You're going to be all right. It won't be long.'

But Barry didn't reply and

she could see that his mouth was caked with mud.

Then he began to choke.

As they dragged Barry out of the clinging earth, Kerry saw the half-buried snout. 'There's a dead badger there, too.'

Tim gazed down, shaking his head, unable to understand.

As Paul gently laid his son on the ground and one of the protestors arrived with a blanket, Barry gazed up at Kerry, still clutching the photograph of his mother. 'There was fresh air,' he croaked. 'They gave me fresh air.'

'Who did?' demanded Paul.

'The badgers, of course.' The whisper was so faint that Kerry wasn't sure if anyone else had heard.

CHAPTER TWELVE

When Barry came home from hospital after lunch the next day, with severe bruising to his neck and back, Kerry sat on the edge of his bed, waiting to break the good news.

'I'd like him to hear it from you,' her uncle had said earlier.

'I should have stopped him going into that hole,' Kerry had begun, needing to confess her stupidity.

But Paul had only looked away impatiently, and her mother had said, 'We can't always stop people doing things. They have to learn in their own way.'

Now Kerry was handing Barry the hastily scribbled note which read:

DEAR BARRY,

    I'VE DECIDED AGAINST CUTTING THE WOOD DOWN. FORTUNATELY, PERMISSION FROM THE COUNCIL'S JUST COME THROUGH FOR A CAMP-SITE IN THE BIG FIELD BY THE ROAD. THIS WILL BRING ME IN ENOUGH CASH. SO THE BADGERS ARE SAFE. I HOPE YOU'RE FEELING BETTER.

    YOURS SINCERELY,

    ANDREW MASON

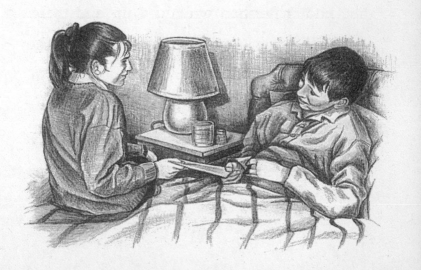

Barry leant back, so visibly relieved that Kerry had to blink away the tears.

'Do you have to go back to London?' he asked.

'We're going to stay a few more days. Until you're better.' Kerry paused and then asked the question that had been puzzling her for so long. 'What was that dead badger doing down there with you? And what was it you said about the badgers giving you fresh air?'

'The corpse was buried.' Barry began to explain about the burial chamber. 'Luckily they hadn't finished walling it up and there was still some fresh air coming in.' He paused, exhausted, and then asked, 'Why don't you come and watch the badgers with me again? Soon.'

Kerry turned to the window, watching the

wood in the fading light as a breeze ruffled the foliage.

'I'd like to,' she said.

A strange joy filled her – a joy she had never experienced before and with it came renewed confidence. She'd made a friend, in spite of all the difficulties. Now, when she went home, Kerry was sure she could make others.

'Mum's going to be buried next week – just like that badger.' Barry spoke slowly and thoughtfully. 'At first I couldn't bear to think she was dead. It was as if she'd been wiped out. I kept trying to hang on to anything that reminded me of her.' His voice broke. 'Now I know she'll always be with me. Wherever I am.' Barry looked up at her and Kerry could see he knew she understood. He had reached out to her at last and they would always be friends.

There was a long silence which Kerry didn't want to break. Instead, she remembered being mist on the bark of a tree. Maybe the dead were like that.